Enid Blyton's
TELL-A-STORY BOOK

The Snow-White Pigeon
and other stories

Mister Quink's Garden

ONCE upon a time, not very long ago, Mr. Brown took his family for a day in the country. There were Mrs. Brown, the mother, Annie Brown, the little girl, and Tommy Brown, the little boy.

"We'll all go, every one of us," said Mr. Brown. "The country is lovely now. We shall enjoy it. Take food enough for the whole day, Mother."

So Mrs. Brown cut ham sandwiches and tomato sandwiches, and packed them into cardboard boxes. She took two bottles of lemon barley water. She packed four oranges and four bananas into a basket with the bottles. She took a large tin of fruit salad, and four cardboard plates and spoons to eat it with. And last of all she took four bars of chocolate and a bag of peppermints.

So you can see that the Brown family meant to have a good feast. It was a lovely day when they set off in the bus. The sun shone brightly. The sky was as blue as the bluebells that were beginning to peep in the woods. The birds in the hedges sang gaily, and the banks were yellow with primroses.

Mrs. Brown was happy. She sat in the bus and

looked at everything. Mr. Brown got out his packet of cigarettes and lighted one. He was happy too. The children looked out for an ice-cream man with his cart, for they each had pennies to spend and they wanted ice-cream. They were happy too.

They got off the bus at last and walked into the woods. The sun was so hot that they were glad of the shade. Tommy and Annie danced on in front, shouting to their mother to look at the bluebells. Mr. and Mrs. Brown carried the bags and basket.

"Look for a nice place to sit, Annie," called Mrs. Brown.

Presently they found one. It was the prettiest place in the wood—and, although they did not know it, it was really the garden belonging to Mister Quink, the old brownie. He lived in the old oak tree under whose branches the Brown family sat. He had a close-fitting door in the trunk of the tree and a small window with a tiny curtain of moss. Nobody ever knew he lived there—except the Little Folk of course—for Mister Quink never showed himself to ordinary people.

Now Mister Quink was very proud of his garden and he worked there every night. There was a tiny stream running through it, and he had planted neatly along each side. He had arranged cushions of moss here and there in his garden too, so that his friends might sit on them when they came to visit him. He had three patches of bluebells, the finest in the wood—and one special secret plant which always grew a *white* bluebell, which, as you know, is a very lucky flower.

Mister Quink had made a little bower of honeysuckle leaves in one corner, and a nook of violets grew close by, so that whoever sat in the nook could smell the sweet scent of the hidden violets. Everything in the garden was neat and tidy and beautiful.

No wonder the Browns thought it was lovely! Mr. and Mrs. Brown sat down under the tree and put their basket and bags by them. They didn't know they were in a brownie's garden, because Mister Quink had no fence or wall or hedge round it. The children wanted to have something to eat at once.

"Well, we'll have our dinner now," said Mrs. Brown, and she began to unpack the things. Soon they were all munching happily. They drank the lemon barley water. It was delicious.

"Let's put the bottles up over there and throw stones at them," said Mr. Brown.

"But won't the broken pieces be dangerous?" said Mrs. Brown.

"Pooh! Who will ever come here?" said Mr. Brown.

So they set up the bottles and threw stones at them, and soon the two bottles were smashed to bits, and pieces of glass lay all over the little dell. Mr. Brown unfolded his newspaper. "Now I'm going to have a smoke and a rest," he said. "Don't disturb me, children.

Little by little the lovely garden belonging to

Mister Quink began to look dreadful. The brownie peeped out of his tiny window in the oak tree and saw with dismay all that was happening.

He saw Mrs. Brown peel oranges for the children and throw the peel on the grass. He saw the children eating bananas and throwing the skins at one another—for they were not very well-behaved children. He saw Mr. Brown throw his empty cigarette packet into the honeysuckle bower.

The Brown family stayed there all the afternoon. It was so peaceful, and the birds sang so sweetly. They had their tea there too—and soon it was time to go home.

Mrs. Brown looked round at the mess, and couldn't help feeling a bit sorry about it.

"Are there any litter-bins or baskets anywhere?" she asked. "Perhaps we ought to put this mess into one."

"There aren't any, Mother," said Tommy. "This is quite a wild part of the wood. I don't suppose anyone comes here but us. All the same, our teacher always tells us at school not to spoil the country—do you suppose we ought to take our rubbish back home with us?"

"I'm not carrying back all that litter," said Mr. Brown at once. He was rather a selfish man. "Leave it here. No one will ever know."

"Mother, let's take these bluebells home with us," cried Annie. "And let's dig up these primroses and violets by the root, and some of this moss.

They'll do fine in our garden at home!"

So they dug up Mister Quink's finest primroses and violets and moss, and picked all his bluebells— and then they found the lucky white bluebell! So they dug up its bulb and put that in the basket too. Then home they went.

Mister Quink opened his front door and crept out. When he saw his beautiful garden scattered with broken glass, orange-peel, banana skins, card-board boxes, empty bags and packets, chocolate paper and sheets of newspaper—when he saw his lovely plants gone and his moss spoilt, he sat down on a stone and cried big tears.

But when he found his white bluebell gone he was very angry! He called a meeting of all the brownies in the wood and they came to see his spoilt garden.

Most of them had complaints and grumbles too.

"Some people left all their horrid paper bags in my field the other day," said Nod, an old brownie.

"And some boys threw broken bottles into my stream, and I cut my feet when I paddled there," said Doolin, a small, bright-eyed brownie.

"But these Browns are the worst of the lot," said Mister Quink fiercely. "Look at this mess! What-ever shall I do with it?"

"The Browns have a neat little garden," said Hoodle, a sharp-eyed brownie who travelled a good deal. "As all this mess belongs to them, why not take it back to them and put it into their own garden?"

"That's a good idea!" said all the brownies at once. "They don't seem to mind litter and rubbish and mess—so maybe they won't bother about broken bottles and papers and peel in their own garden."

"I can give them about six old newspapers I've picked up from my field at one time and another," said Nod.

"And I can give them a sackful of broken glass," said Doolin.

"We'll go tonight and dump everything in the Browns' garden," said everyone. "Just the thing! How pleased they will be to get such a nice lot of rubbish back!"

So that night seven brownies all made their way from the wood and rode on the back of the midnight owl who flies to and from the town. When they got to the Browns' garden they landed on the grass and opened their sacks.

They shook out the glass all over the neat lawn. They threw the newspapers where the wind could blow them around. They scatterd the paper and boxes and peel and skin here and there. And just as they were going, Mister Quink stopped short and pointed to something.

"Look!" he said. "My lucky white bluebell! I must take that back with me."

"And see—here's a lupin plant just flowering!" said Nod. "I haven't one of those at home. As the Browns took your flowers, Quink, they probably wouldn't mind us taking theirs. I *must* have that lupin!"

In a few minutes the brownies were digging up all the finest things in the Brown's garden, and then off they went again on the owl, their sacks empty of rubbish but full now of lovely plants. The brownies were delighted.

In the morning, when Mr. Brown awoke and looked out of the window to see what sort of a day it was, he got *such* a shock! His garden was a perfect wreck! His pet plants were gone—his lawn was scattered with broken glass—and all kinds of rubbish blew about or lay on the beds.

"Just look at that!" said Mr. Brown fiercely. "Just look at that. Now who's done that, I should like to know!"

Mrs. Brown jumped out of bed and gazed at the dreadful garden. Tears came into her eyes, for she loved her little garden. "Oh, how could anyone be so horrid!" she said.

Tommy and Annie were angry too. "What a terrible mess," said Annie. "Why don't people clear up their litter properly instead of throwing it into *our* garden?"

Well, Mr. Brown told the policeman, and the policeman wrote a lot of things down in his notebook and said he would keep a watch in the garden and see it didn't happen again. And Tommy and Annie spent the whole morning clearing up the mess and making the garden neat. Mr. Brown had to buy more plants in place of the ones that had gone, and he was very angry about it.

Well, will you believe it, although the policeman watched carefully the next night, *some*body he didn't see came and emptied all sorts of rubbish in the Browns' garden again! It was most extraordinary because although the policeman saw the rubbish being thrown about the garden he couldn't see who was throwing it!

The brownies were invisible to him, for he didn't believe in fairies. He was frightened and ran all the way back to the police-station.

And do you know, the brownies still come every other night or so and give to the Browns all the rubbish that people leave about the countryside. Their garden is a dreadful sight and they can't do anything about it.

Annie is beginning to wonder if it *can* be the Little Folk who are doing it—and she wishes the Browns hadn't been so untidy in the wood that day!

"I shall put up a notice to say we're sorry and won't spoil the country again," said Annie to herself. "Then the Little Folk will stop bringing us rubbish."

So she is going to do that tonight—and then the brownies will have to choose someone else's garden. I hope it won't be yours! But I'm sure you are not like the Browns, are you? You know how to behave when you go the country, so *your* garden will be safe!

Mollie's Mud Pies

IT was very hot, so hot that Mollie wore only a sunsuit. It was nearly summer, and Mummy said if it was so hot now, whatever would it be like in the middle of summer.

"It's nice," said Mollie, who liked wearing almost nothing. She didn't even wear shoes in the garden. "I like it, Mummy. I do wish we were by the sea, then I could bathe."

"Well, I'll tell you what I will do," said her mother. "I will water you each night before you go to bed!"

"Water me!" said Mollie, in surprise. "What do you mean, Mummy?"

"Just what I say," said Mummy. "I'll fill a can with half-warm water, and then water you before you go to bed. That will be fun for you."

"Oh, *yes*," said Mollie in delight. "I should love that."

She played in the hot garden. The grass looked yellow, not green. Everywhere was dried up and dusty. Mollie wondered if the birds had any puddles to drink from. They must be thirsty now, with all the puddles dried up. So she filled a little bowl with water, and set it out on the grass. It was fun to see the birds coming to drink from it.

"They drink so sweetly," said Mollie. "They dip in their beaks, and then hold their heads back, Mummy, and let the water run down their throats."

When the evening came, Mummy filled a big watering-can with half-warm water, and called Mollie. "Come and have your watering!"

"Will it make me grow, like the flowers?" cried Mollie, dancing about. Mummy tipped up the can. Mollie gave a squeal. Although the water was not cold, it felt cold on her hot little body. She danced about, squeaking with excitement and joy.

"The water's made a nice muddy patch on the path," she cried. "Look, my toes are brown and muddy with dancing in it."

"You'll have to wash them well," said Mummy, filling the can again. "Come along—one more watering and you must go to bed."

The patch of path was indeed wet and muddy after the second can of water had been poured all over Mollie. "If it's wet tomorrow, I shall make little mud pies of it," said Mollie.

It was still muddy the next day. After breakfast Mollie went to the mud and dabbled her fingers in it. "I shall make little pies and cakes of mud, and set them in the sun to dry," she thought. "That will be a nice game to play."

Mummy called her. "If you want to play that dirty game you must wear an overall over that nice clean sun-suit. Come along."

Mollie ran indoors. When she came out again she

found someone else in her mud-patch! It was a little bird with a touch of white at the foot of his dark, long tail, and underneath his body. He stared at Mollie, and then scraped up some mud in his beak.

"Oh!" said Mollie, pleased. "Are you making mud-pies too? I never knew a bird liked playing with mud before. Do play with me."

The little bird gave a twitter, filled his beak quite full, and then suddenly darted into the air on curving wings. Mollie saw that he had a forked tail behind him.

"I wish he hadn't gone," she thought. "It would have been fun to play with him. I suppose he has taken the mud to make mud-pies somewhere else."

Suddenly the little bird came back again. He looked at Mollie, and she looked at him. He wondered if Mollie was the kind of child to throw stones at him, or to shout and frighten him away.

But she wasn't. She was like you. She liked birds, and wanted them to stay close to her so that she could watch them and make friends with them.

She sat quite still and watched him. He went to the mud again, and began to scrape up some more. Then another bird, exactly like him, flew down, and he began to dabble in it as well. Mollie was delighted.

"Everyone is making mud-pies this morning," she said. "Gracious—here's another! How busy they all are in my muddy patch. I'll get busy too."

Once the birds had made up their minds that

Mollie was a friend, they became very busy indeed. They filled their little beaks with mud time after time, and then flew away round the house Mollie wondered where they went. They kept coming and going all the morning.

"Funny little mud-pie birds," she said to them. "Do you bake your mud-pies up on the roof somewhere? I bake mine here, look!"

The hot sun baked her pies beautifully. She put them on a plate out of her tea-set and took them in to her Mummy.

"Have a mud-pie?" she said. "They are lovely. And, oh, Mummy, the mud-pie birds have played in the mud with me all morning. They were sweet."

Mummy was surprised. "Mud-pie birds! Whatever do you mean?"

"Well, they came and played with my mud and took some away to make mud-pies with. I expect they baked them up on the roof," said Mollie.

Mummy thought it was a little tale of Mollie's. She pretended to eat Mollie's mud-pie, and then offered Mollie a bun from the oven.

"I've been baking too," she said. "Have a hot bun? And now I think you had better stop playing with the mud and wash yourself."

"The mud is gone now," said Mollie. "The sun has baked it hard."

The little birds didn't come into the garden any more that day. "I suppose they only came for the mud," thought Mollie. "Well, if Mummy waters me again tonight there will be more mud tomorrow for us all to play with."

There was—a nice big patch—and down came the little birds again, to scrape up the mud. Mollie was so pleased.

"It's nice to have you to play with me," she said to the busy little birds. "But I really wish you would tell me what you do with your mud."

They twittered a little song to her, high and sweet, but she didn't understand what they said. They flew to and from the mud all morning, till the sun dried it up.

"Mummy, why do the mud-pie birds take my mud?" asked Mollie. "I do want to know. I didn't know that birds like mud so much."

Her Daddy was there, and he looked up from his newspaper. "What's all this about mud-pie birds?" he asked. So Mollie told him.

"Ah," he said. "Now I know what birds you mean. Your mud-pie birds are house-martins, cousins of the pretty swallows we see flying high in the air all summer."

"House-martins!" said Mollie. "*I* should call them mud-martins. What do they do with my mud?"

"Come with me and I'll show you," said Daddy. He took Mollie's hand, and led her upstairs. They went into her bedroom. Daddy went to the window and opened it wide.

"Now look out of your window, above it, to the

edge of the roof overhead," he said. "Tell me what you see."

Mollie leaned out, and looked up. She gave a cry. "Oh, Daddy! The mud-pie birds are there. They are making something of my mud. What is it?"

"It's a nest," said Daddy. "The house-martins don't use dead leaves and twigs and moss for their nests as most birds do. They make them of mud. They fetch beakfuls of mud, and plaster it against the wall, gradually building it out till they have made a fine nest of mud, with a hole to get in and out. There's the hole in that nest. Look!"

As Mollie watched, one of the little birds flew up with his beak full of mud from somewhere, and presed it against the edge of his nest.

"There you are," said Daddy. "He brings wet mud, and it dries hard in the sun, making a perfectly good nest for his little wife to lay her eggs in, and have her young ones."

"Oh Daddy! Fancy making a nest of my mud, the mud that was made when Mummy watered me each evening," said Mollie in delight. "I couldn't think why the mud-birds came to make mud-pies. I did not know they were making mud-nests—and over my bedroom window, too, tucked under the edge of the roof! I shall hear them calling and twittering to each other all day long. Look—there's another nest farther along. You won't pull them down, will you?"

"Of course not!" said Daddy, who was fond of

birds. "They can nest there in peace and happiness, out of reach of the cats. Later on we shall see their young ones popping their heads out of the holes in the mud-nests."

And so they did! The house-martins laid eggs in their queer mud-nests, and in a few weeks' time Mollie saw three or four tiny feathery heads popping out of the hole in the nest above her window, waiting for the father and mother to come back with flies to feed them.

Later still the little birds flew into the sky with their mother and father, learning how to dart and soar and glide, and how to catch the hundreds of insects that flew in the air. Daddy said they did a great deal of good, because the flies were a pest.

And then one day they were all gone. Mollie looked into the sky and they were not there.

"They've gone away south, where it is warmer," said Daddy. "There will be plenty of insects for them to eat there. Our winter is coming and they do not like that."

"I don't want them to go away," said Mollie sadly.

"Well, they will be back again in the spring," said Daddy. "And, Mollie, if the weather is hot and dry again when they come back, you must make a muddy patch once more, and they will come to it, and build their nest again over your window. They love to come back to exactly the same place, if they can."

So, of course, Mollie is going to watch for them when the spring-time comes. You must watch too, and if we have hot and dry weather in May, when the mud-pie birds want to build their nests, you can do as Mollie did—make a muddy patch for them, and watch them fly down to it to fill their beaks.

Maybe they will build a mud-nest over your window, too. That really would be fun, wouldn't it?

The Ugly Old Toad

ONCE upon a time a big old toad wanted to cross the road to get to a pond he knew on the other side. He couldn't jump high and quickly like his cousin the frog. He could only do small hops, or crawl, but he set off valiantly, hoping to get across the road before anything came along.

He was almost across when a horse and cart came down the lane. Clippitty-cloppitty, clippitty-cloppitty went the horse's hoofs, and the old toad heard them. He tried to hop away quickly, but one of the horse's hoofs trod on his back leg. Almost at once the horse lifted his hoof again and went on, not knowing that he had crushed the foot of the toad.

"Oh!" groaned the toad to himself, crawling to the side of the road, dragging his hurt foot behind him. "What a bit of bad luck! I can hardly walk now. How my foot is hurting me!"

He was in such pain that he could not go any farther. He squatted by the side of the road, hoping that his foot would soon get better. But it didn't.

He tried again to crawl, but his foot hurt him too much, so he lay there, half-hidden by a tuft of grass, hoping that no enemy would come by.

The big rat ran by, and stopped when he saw the toad. "Aha! Dinner for me!" thought the rat, knowing that the toad was hurt. He ran up to the toad and snapped at him.

The toad still could not crawl away, but he had a good trick to play on the rat. He oozed out an evil-smelling, horrible-tasting liquid all over his back. When the rat tried to bite him, he got his mouth full of the nasty stuff.

"Horrible!" said the rat, and stood staring at the toad with his mouth open, trying to let the nasty-tasting stuff drip out of his mouth. "Horrible! I wouldn't have *you* for my dinner for anything!"

He ran off, and the toad sat still, glad to be rid of him. Then he heard footsteps coming down the lane, and he shrank back into the grass, trying to look like a brown clod of earth. He really did look like one.

Soon a boy came up, whistling. He almost trod on the toad, but he did not see him and went whistling on. He thought the old toad was just a lump of earth. That was another of the toad's tricks—to make himself like a clod of earth.

He sat on, still hoping that his foot would stop hurting. But the horse's hoof had been hard and heavy—it was a wonder it had not cut the toad's foot right off.

Then the toad heard more footsteps—lighter ones this time. He crouched down again, but this time the passer-by was sharper-eyed than the boy had been.

"Ooh! A toad!" said a voice, and the toad, looking up cautiously, saw a little girl gazing down at him. She wrinkled her nose in disgust.

25

"Nasty creature! I can't bear toads! Ugly thing with your pimply back and your creepy-crawly ways! I don't like you a bit!"

The toad crouched very still. He was afraid. This little girl might stamp on him—children were sometimes very cruel to creatures like him. But he couldn't help being an ugly old toad—he was born like that.

However, the little girl did not stamp on him. She wasn't cruel. She did think the toad was ugly, and she didn't like him, but she wasn't going to be unkind.

"I don't like ugly creatures," she said to the toad. "I couldn't bear to touch you. Oooh, that *would* be horrid! It would make me feel ill."

The toad was sad. He wished he had been born a butterfly or a bird. Then perhaps the little girl would have liked him. But you had to be what you were born to be—there wasn't any help for it.

Then suddenly the little girl saw the toad's foot. It was all crushed and flattened. She stared at it in horror.

"Toad! Your foot is squashed to bits! Is it hurting you? Oh, how did that happen? Did someone tread on you?"

The toad still crouched flat. He knew the little girl wouldn't tread on him now, but he was still afraid. She looked at him, sad because of his foot.

"Oh, I can't leave you here like this," she said. "I'm sorry I said all those unkind things now. I didn't know you were hurt. I think I had better take you home to my mother—she will know what to do with your foot."

The toad didn't want to be taken home. He wanted to be left alone in peace. The little girl was wondering how to carry him.

"Although I am very sorry for you, I simply *can't* touch you," she said. "I can't! I should drop you if I touched you. You see, I don't like toads."

Then she thought of her handkerchief. She would wrap the toad in that and carry him by taking hold of the four corners of the hanky. Then she would not need to touch him at all.

So to the toad's surprise and fright, she dropped her hanky over him, rolled him gently into it, and picked him up in the hanky. She carried him by taking hold of the four corners, but she didn't even like doing that!

She took him home. The toad did not wriggle or struggle, becaue it hurt his foot too much. He just lay in the hanky, very miserable, wondering what was going to happen to him.

The little girl went in at her gate. She called to her mother. "Mummy! I've got a hurt toad. Can you do something for him?"

Her mother was very surprised. She undid the hanky and took the toad in her bare hands. She didn't mind touching any creature. She saw the hurt foot and was sorry.

"I can't do much," she said. "I will just bathe it

with very weak iodine—but it's no good binding it up. The best thing you can do for him, Jenny, is to put him in a cool, shady corner of the garden, where there are plenty of flies for him to catch, and leave him to himself. Maybe the foot will heal itself."

"I don't like him much," said Jenny.

"He can't help being a toad," said her mother. "*You* might have been born a toad—and think how sad you would be if people hated you, and tried to hurt you because you happened to be ugly. That's not fair, Jenny."

"No, it isn't," said Jenny. She looked down at the toad, and he looked up at her. She saw his eyes.

"Mummy, he's got the most beautiful eyes!" she said surprised. "Do look at them. They are like jewels in his head, gleaming as bright as copper."

"All toads have lovely eyes," said Mummy. "They are nice creatures, Jenny, and make good pets."

"Oh, *no*, Mummy!" said Jenny, astonished. "I have never heard of a toad as a pet before!"

"There are quite a lot of things you haven't heard of!" said Mummy. "Now—I've finished bathing his foot—do you think you can possibly bring yourself to carry him in your hands to a nice bit of the garden—or do you dislike toads so much?"

Jenny felt a bit ashamed of herself. She looked down at the toad. His coppery eyes gleamed kindly at her. He looked patient and wise.

"I'll carry him," she said, and she picked him up

gently in her hands. He kept quite still. Jenny took him down the garden and put him in the cool hedge behind Daddy's lettuces.

"There you are!" she said. "Stay there and catch flies. I don't know what else you eat, but there are heaps of flies here for you."

There were. The toad heard a big one buzzing just over his head. He looked at it—and then, quick as a flash, he shot out a long sticky tongue, caught the fly on the tip of it, swallowed, and looked at Jenny.

"A good meal," he seemed to say. Jenny laughed.

"You're rather nice," she said, and left him.

She forgot all about him. A week went by, then two weeks. Then Daddy came in one evening, bringing two delicious lettuces for supper.

"Good gracious!" said Mummy, pleased. "I thought you told me that all your lettuces had been eaten by slugs, Daddy. What beauties these are!"

"Ah! I've got someone to guard my lettuces for me!" said Daddy. "And a very good fellow he is, too. He never allows a single slug on my lettuce-bed now."

"Who is he?" said Jenny, puzzled.

"He's a toad," said Daddy, "a wise, friendly, kind old toad. He lives in the hedge behind my kitchen garden, and he keeps guard over the lettuces. See how well they have grown since the old toad looked after them for me!"

"Daddy! He must be *my* toad! I forgot all about

him," said Jenny, excited.

"*Your* toad? I thought you didn't like toads," said Daddy. "What do you mean?"

Jenny told him. "And we shall know if it *is* my toad by his foot," she said. "Has he got a mended foot, Daddy?"

"I didn't notice," said Daddy. "Let's go and see."

So they went to see—and there was the old toad, and behind him was his hurt foot—mended and healed now, but rather a funny shape.

"It *is* my toad!" said Jenny. "Look, he's crawling over to me, Daddy. He knows I'm the little girl who brought him home."

"Tickle his back with a grass," said Daddy. "He'll like that."

So Jenny did, and the toad liked it very much. He tried to scratch his back with one of his feet, and made Jenny laugh.

"You're a good old toad," she said. "I like you, and you shall be my pet."

He *is* her pet, and he still keeps guard over the kitchen garden. I know because I've seen him there!

The Snow-white Pigeon

ONCE upon a time there was a little girl called Isabel.

She was very fond of birds and animals, but she hadn't any of her own, not even a tortoise. So she made the wild birds her pets, and fed them every day, putting the crumbs and scraps on an old tree-stump in the garden.

One day a snow-white pigeon flew down to feed with the other birds. Isabel was surprised.

"Look, Mummy," she said. "There's a fan-tail pigeon—see its beautiful fan-like tail. I wonder where it has come from. I do wish I could have one for my own."

But Isabel's mother was very poor, and she could not even afford the few pence for the corn that the pigeon would have to eat. So she shook her head.

"We have no money for pets," she said. "Pigeons eat corn, Isabel. That one which flew down to feed is not eating anything. It just flew down to see if there was any seed or corn there—but now that it finds none it will fly away."

The pigeon *would* have flown away—but suddenly something dreadful happened. The next-door cat came creeping along, hid behind a bush—and then jumped out at the poor white pigeon!

"Oh! Oh!" screamed Isabel in a fright, and she rushed out at once. She scared away the cat, and ran to lift up the hurt pigeon.

One of its wings had been bitten, and it could not fly. It was very frightened, and its ruby-red eyes were shut. Isabel gently carried the pigeon to her mother.

"It will be all right in a day or two," said her mother. "It must be kept in a cage until it can fly again, or the cat will get it once more."

"I haven't a cage," said Isabel, frowning. Then she cheered up. "But, Mother, what about that old rabbit-hutch in the shed? Would that do?"

"Yes, if you clean it out," said Mother. "You can easily keep the pigeon there for a little while. We must find out whom it belongs to, and they can have their pigeon back when its wing is better."

So Isabel cleaned out the old rabbit-hutch and mended the wire in front with string. Then she set it out in the garden by the dining-room window. She gently placed the hurt pigeon into the old hutch.

Mother had washed its wing, and the pigeon had its eyes open now. It was stil frightened, but it did not mind Isabel's gentle hands. It knew that the little girl loved it.

"Mother, what shall I feed it on?" asked Isabel. "I haven't a penny for some corn."

"Run down to the farmer's wife and see if she

wants any errands done," said Mother. "Maybe she would give you a handful of corn if you help her a bit."

So off went Isabel, and asked Mrs. Straw, the farmer's wife, if there was any work she could do.

"Yes," said Mrs. Straw at once. "You can wash all the eggs for me, ready for market. I haven't time this morning. Mind you don't break any!"

Isabel washed nearly a hundred eggs and didn't break a single one. Mrs. Straw was pleased.

"You can have three eggs to take home," she said. But Isabel looked at her shyly.

"Do you think I might have a handful of corn instead?" she asked. "I've a hurt pigeon, and I've no food for it."

"Bless the child! Of course you can take the corn!" said Mrs. Straw, and she bustled off to see to her baking. Isabel ran to the corn bin and took a handful of corn. Then, holding it in her overall so that she shouldn't waste even a grain, she went slowly back home. The pigeon was simply delighted with the corn, for it was very hungry.

"Rookity-coo, rookity-coo!" it said to Isabel, and pecked up the corn as quickly as it could. By the morning there was no corn left.

"I'll have to go and do a few more jobs for Mrs. Straw," said Isabel. "Then perhaps she will give me some more corn."

So off she went. Mrs. Straw was pleased to see her, for the little girl was a good worker.

"Good morning," she said. "You are just in time. I've six baby lambs in the farm-garden that I am bringing up by hand. Will you heat their milk for me, put it into these babies' bottles, and then feed all the lambs, one by one?"

Well, wasn't that a lovely job to do? Isabel was delighted. She heated the milk in a big saucepan on Mrs. Straw's oil-stove, and then she filled the bottles. She made them cooler for the lambs, and then went out to feed them. The long-legged creatures came frisking up to her, greedy and hungry. One by one she fed them, putting the teat of the bottle into their mouths, and letting them suck out the warm milk.

"This is a lovely thing to do," sighed Isabel happily. "Dear little lambs. I can't believe you grow into those fat old sheep!"

Mrs. Straw was pleased with Isabel for helping her again. "Take six apples home for yourself," she said. "There are some in the store-room."

Isabel would dearly have liked the apples, but she wanted some corn for the pigeon. Mrs. Straw nodded and said Yes, she could take another handful if she liked. So Isabel took home another handful and fed the hungry pigeon.

She looked into the cage, where the pigeon was comfortably sitting on the hay. When the fan-tail walked over to the corn, Isabel saw something on the hay.

"It's an egg," she cried, "a pretty white egg! The

34

pigeon has laid it. Oh, I wonder if a baby pigeon will come out of it!"

She ran to tell her mother. Mother was so surprised.

"Well, well!" she said. "Who would have thought of that?"

"I do wonder whom the pigeon belongs to," said Isabel. "They will be surprised to know that it has laid an egg."

"I have found out who the owner is," said Mother. "It is Miss Kennedy, down the lane. She has lost one. You can go and tell her, if you like, that you have her pigeon safely."

So off went Isabel and saw Miss Kennedy, who was a very kind lady indeed, just as fond of birds and animals as Isabel was.

"A cat hurt your pigeon," said Isabel, "so I put it into an old hutch and looked after it. I hadn't any pennies to buy corn, so I did some jobs for Mrs. Straw, and she let me have some corn for the pigeon. And now it has laid an egg!"

"Well, you *have* been a kind little friend to my hurt pigeon," said Miss Kennedy. "Will you keep it for me until the egg has hatched and the baby is old enough to look after itself? Perhaps you would like to keep the baby and have it for your own pigeon? I can always give you some of my corn for it!"

Isabel was so delighted that she could hardly say thank you. To have a pigeon of her very own—one that she had had from an egg! It was too lovely for anything.

She raced back to tell the good news to Mother. Mother was pleased too, because she knew how much Isabel would love a pet of her own.

The pigeon sat day after day on its white egg. its wing healed, but Isabel did not let it fly out, in case the cat got it again. Not until the egg was hatched and the queer little baby was old enough to see to itself did she open the hutch and let the mother-pigeon fly back to Miss Kennedy's pigeon-house.

But the baby-pigeon always stayed with Isabel, and grew big and white and beautiful like its mother. It had a wonderful fan-tail that it spread out when it walked. It said, "Rookity-coo, rookity-coo!" to Isabel whenever it saw her.

She has the pigeon still— and guess what she has called it! I wonder if you guessed right? Well, she called it Snow White!

The Witch's Cat

OLD Dame Kirri was a witch. You could tell she was because she had bright green eyes. She was a good witch, though, and spent most of her time making good spells to help people who were ill or unhappy.

She lived in Toppling Cottage, which was just like its name, and looked exactly as if it were going to topple over. But it was kept up by strong magic, and not a brick had fallen, although the cottage was five hundred years old.

At the back of the cottage was the witch's garden. Round it ran a very, very high wall, taller than the tallest man.

"I like a high wall. It keeps people from peeping and prying," said the old witch Kirri. "In my garden I grow a lot of strange and powerful herbs. I don't want people to see them and steal them. I won't have people making spells from my magic herbs—they might make bad ones."

The witch had a cat. It was black and big, and had green eyes very like the witch's. Its name was Cinder-Boy.

Cinder-Boy helped the witch in her spells. He was really a remarkably clever cat. He knew how to sit exactly in the middle of a chalk ring without moving, whilst Kirri the witch danced round and sang spells. He knew how to go out and collect

dew-drops in the moonlight. He took a special little silver cup, and never spilt a drop.

He never drank milk. He liked tea, made as strong as the witch made her own. Sometimes he would sit and sip his tea and purr, and the witch would sip *her* tea, and purr too. It was funny to see them

Cinder-Boy loved to sleep in the walled-in garden. He knew all the flowers and herbs there. No weed was allowed to grow. Cinder-Boy scratched them all up.

But one day he came to a small plant growing at the foot of the wall. It had leaves like a rose-tree, and pale-pink flowers with a mass of yellow stamens in the middle. It smelt very sweet.

"What flower are you?" said Cinder-Boy. "You smell rather like a rose."

"Well, that's just what I am," said the plant. "I'm a wild rose."

"How did you get in here?" said Cinder-Boy, surprised.

"A bird dropped a seed," said the wild rose. "But I don't like being here, black cat."

"My name is Cinder-Boy," said the witch's cat. "Why don't you like being here? It is a very nice place to be."

"Well, I feel shut in." said the wild rose. "I'm not very large. If I were taller than the wall I could grow up into the air and see over the top. I don't like being down here at the bottom, shut in."

"Well, grow tall, then," said Cinder-Boy. "I can give you a spell to make your stems nice and long, if you like. Then you can reach up to the top of the wall and look over. There's a nice view there, I can tell you."

"Oh, would you do that?" said the wild rose in delight. "Thank you!"

So Cinder-Boy went off to get a spell to make the stems of the wild rose grow very long. He soon found one. It was in a small blue bottle, and he poured it into a watering-can. The spell was blue too.

Then he watered the wild rose with the spell, and it began to work almost at once. In two or three days the stems of the wild rose had grown quite high into the air.

"Go on growing. You will soon be at the top of the wall!" said Cinder-Boy.

So the wild rose went on making its stems longer and longer, hoping to get to the very top of the wall.

But when next Cinder-Boy strolled out into the garden to see how it was getting on, what a shock he had. Every single stem was bent over and lay sprawling over the grass!

"What has happened?" said Cinder-Boy, waving his tail in surprise.

"My stalks grew tall, but they didn't grow stong," said the wild rose sadly. "Just as I reached the top of the wall, they all flopped over and fell down. They are not strong enough to bear their own weight."

"Well, how do plants with weak stems manage to climb high then?" said Cinder-Boy, puzzled. "Runner beans grow high, and they have very weak stems. Sweet-peas grow high, and they have weak stems too. I'll go and see how they do it."

So off he went, for the witch grew both in her garden. He soon came back.

"The beans twine their stalks around poles," he said, "and the sweet-peas grow little green fingers, called tendrils, which catch hold of things, and they pull themselves up high like that. Can't you do that?"

The wild rose couldn't. It didn't know how to. Its stems wouldn't twist themselves, however much it tried to make them do so; and it couldn't grow a tendril at all.

"Well, we must think of another way," said the cat.

"Cinder-Boy, how do *you* get up to the top of the wall?" asked the wild rose. "You are often up there in the sun. I see you. Well, how do *you* get to the top?"

"I run up the trees," said Cinder-Boy. "Do you see the young fruit trees near you? Well, I run up those to the top of the wall. I use my claws to help me. I dig them into the bark of the trees, and hold on with them."

He showed the wild rose his big curved claws. "I can put them in or out, as I like," he said. "They are very useful claws."

The wild rose thought they were too. "If I grew claws like that I could easily climb up the fruit trees, right through them to the top, and then I'd be waving at the top of the wall," it said. "Can't you get me some claws like yours, Cinder-Boy?"

The cat blinked his green eyes and thought hard. "I know what I could do," he said. "I could ask the witch Kirri, my mistress, to make some magic claws that would grow on you. I'll ask her today. In return you must promise to grow her some lovely scarlet hips, berries that she can trim her hats and bonnets with in the autumn."

"Oh, I will, I will," promised the wild rose. So Cinder-Boy went off to the witch Kirri, and asked her for what he wanted.

She grumbled a little. "It is difficult to make claws," she said, "very difficult. You will have to help me, Cinder-Boy. You will have to sit in the middle of a blue ring of chalk, and put out all your claws at once, whilst I sing a magic song. Don't be scared at what happens."

Cinder-Boy went to sit in the middle of a chalk ring that the witch drew in the middle of her kitchen floor. He stuck out all his claws as she commanded.

She danced round with her broom-stick, singing such a magic song that Cinder-Boy felt quite scared. Then a funny thing happened. His claws fell out on to the floor with a clatter—and they turned red or green as they fell. He looked at his paws and saw new ones growing. Then those fell out. How very

queer!

Soon there was quite a pile of claws on the floor. Then the witch stopped singing and dancing, and rubbed out the rim of chalk.

"You can come out now, Cinder-Boy," she said. "The magic is finished."

Cinder-Boy collected all the red and green claws. They were strong and sharp. He took them out into the garden, and came to the wild rose.

"I've got the claws for you!" he said. "The witch Kirri did some strong magic. Look, here they are. I'll press each one into your stems, till you have claws all down them. Then I'll say a growing-spell and they will grow into you properly, and belong to you."

So Cinder-Boy did that, and the wild rose felt the cat-claws growing firmly into the long stem.

"Now," said Cinder-Boy in excitement, "now you will be able to climb up through the fruit trees, wild rose. I will help you at first."

So Cinder-Boy took the wild rose stems, all set with claws, and pushed them up into the little fruit tree that grew near by. The claws took hold of the bark and held on firmly. Soon all the stems were climbing up high through the little fruit tree, the claws digging themselves into the trunk and the branches.

The wild rose grew higher. It pulled itself up by its new claws. It was at the top of the wall! It could see right over it to the big world beyond.

"Now I'm happy," said the wild rose to Cinder-Boy. "Come and sit up here on the wall beside me. Let us look at the big world together. Oh, Cinder-Boy, it is lovely up here. I am not shut in any longer. Thank you for my claws. I do hope I shall go on growing them now."

It did. And it grew beautiful scarlet berries in the autumn, for witch Kirri's winter bonnets. You should see how gay the bonnets are when she trims them with the rose hips.

Ever since that day the wild roses have grown cats' claws all down their stems, sometimes green and sometimes red or pink. They use them to climb with. Have you seen them? If you haven't, do go and look. It will surprise you to see cats' claws growing out of a plant!

It was a good idea of Cinder-Boys, wasn't it?

The Tale of Silly-One and Artful

ONCE upon a time Silly-One the pixie went for a picnic all by himself. He had a package of meat sandwiches, some jammy buns, a bar of chocolate and a bottle of lemonade. So he was going to have a very good picnic.

He sat down in a nice place. A small pond was just by him, and a green hedge was behind him. The sun shone on the water and many flies danced about over the pond.

Silly-One opened his packet of sandwiches, and began to eat them. There was a bit of meat in one that he didn't like.

"You taste nasty," said Silly-One, and threw the piece of meat into the pond. It didn't sink, but lay there on the surface.

Silly-One looked for it again in a moment or two and was most surprised to find dozens of tiny black tadpoles feasting on the bit of meat. They were swimming round it, pulling at it, and having a fine time.

"Look at that now," said Silly-One. "I never knew before that tadpoles liked a bit of meat. I'd like to take some of them home and keep them. I could give them a bit of meat every day."

He dipped his hand in the water and tried to catch the tadpoles, but they swam away fast. Silly-One went on with his dinner, and threw another bit of meat into the pond. At once a swarm of little black tadpoles, wriggling their tails behind them, swam to it and feasted on it.

It was fun to watch them. Silly-One looked at them whilst he finished his sandwiches. Then he ate his jammy buns, his bar of chocolate, and drank his lemonade out of the bottle; he had forgotten to bring a cup.

"I'd like to take some of those tadpoles home, I really would," he said, and wondered how to get them. He took the empty lemonade bottle and held it in the pond. As it filled with water several tadpoles swam into it too.

Silly-One was delighted. He took the bottle out of the water and held it up.

"Aha, little taddies—I have six of you!" he said. "I'll take you home and put you into my goldfish bowl and feed you on bits of meat every day. And you'll grow into giant tadpoles, so that I shall have to dig a pond in my garden for you to live in."

He didn't want to go home just then. He stood the bottle in the shade and lay down. "I think I'll have a little nap," he said. "Just a little tiny one."

So he shut his eyes—but very soon he felt something crawling over his face, and he sat up in a hurry. It was a caterpillar!

"Oh—you funny leggy creature," said Silly-One. "Why do you crawl over me? Oh, my goodness, what a lot of you there are on that plant. No wonder you dropped on to my face. I laid down just under you."

He liked the caterpillar. He liked the way it crawled about so quickly on his hand.

"I've a good mind to take you home too," he said. "Yes, I have! I haven't any pets, and I think six tadpoles and six caterpillars would be nice pets. I could dig up the plant you are feeding on, and take that home too. I could put it in a pot and the six of you could feast all day long. How would you like that?"

The caterpillar didn't answer. It seemed in a great hurry.

Silly-One got busy. He dug up the whole plant. He took six caterpillars and popped them into the cardboard sandwich box. He made little holes in he lid so that the caterpillars could breathe.

Then, carrying his bottle of tadpoles in water, his plant, and his box of caterpillars he began to make his way home.

On the way he met Artful the brownie. Artful was always trying to make Silly-One come and live with him and do his work. But Silly-One didn't want to, so he wasn't very pleased to meet Artful on his way home.

"Hallo!" said Artful. "Been for a picnic?"

"Hallo," said Silly-One. "Yes, I have. Good-bye."

"Don't be in such a hurry!" said Artful. "What have you got in that bottle?"

"Tadpoles," said Silly-One. "Good-bye."

"And what have you got in that box?" asked Artful.

"Caterpillars," said Silly-One. "Good-bye."

"Now, look here—anyone would think you wanted to get away from me," said Artful, annoyed.

"I do," said Silly-One. "Good-bye."

Artful was angry. "I think you're a very, very silly pixie," he said. "Here am I, always offering you a good home and wages—if you'll come and do my bit of work for me—and you just won't come. You're silly. Silly by name and silly by nature."

"I may be silly, but I'm not coming," said Silly-One; "and what's more, you can't make me. You don't know enough magic to make a hen lay eggs!"

"Oh, don't I?" cried Artful, in a fine rage. "Well, I'll prove to you I'm a very powerful brownie; I'll use stong magic. I'll frighten you so that you'll come and be my servant in case you get changed into a black beetle or something."

"Pooh," said Silly-One. "Good-bye."

"Now, look here," said Artful, and he caught hold of Silly-One's arm, nearly making him spill his

48

tadpoles. "Now, look here—I'll use my magic, and I'll change those nice wriggly tadpoles of yours into frogs."

"No, don't!" said Silly-One in alarm. "I don't like frogs. They make me jump when they suddenly leap high in the air. Don't you dare use any magic on my tadpoles! Anyway, I don't believe you know enough. It would need very strong magic to turn taddies into frogs."

"And what's more," said Artful, speaking right into Silly-One's ear in a most mysterious way, "and what's more, Silly-One, I'll change those cater-pillars of yours into moths—yellow moths that will flutter round your head and frighten you!"

"You're not to do anything of the sort," said Silly-One. "I don't like moths. Some people do, but I don't. They scare me. I know it's silly, but they just scare me. You leave my caterpillars alone. Any-way, you couldn't do it. You're only boasting. It would need very strong magic to change these leggy caterpillars into beautiful moths, with wings and feelers. Don't be silly!"

"I will, I tell you," said Artful, and he took a little wand out of his pocket. He waved it over the lemonade bottle and over the box of caterpillars.

"Abra-cadabra, abra-cadabra, rimminy-romminy-ree!" he said solemnly. "There! Now they will change into frogs and moths. You'll see, Silly-One. Just a matter of weeks, and you'll know how strong my magic is."

"Good-bye," said Silly-One, and fled. He didn't believe in Artful's magic at all, but it made him feel uncomfortable.

"Don't you worry," he said to his tadpoles, when he filled his old goldfish bowl with water, and popped them in. "Don't you worry. You won't be changed into frogs. Artful's magic is no good."

He put the plant he had brought home into a pot, and then placed the six caterpillars gently on it.

"There," he said, "have a good feast. You are my pets now. You won't be changed into anything. You needn't believe in Artful's silly magic."

Silly-One got fond of his queer pets. He fetched waterweed from the pond for his tadpoles, and he gave them a bit of meat each day. He watered the plant his caterpillars fed on, and was pleased to see them growing bigger and bigger.

Then one day he noticed that his tadpoles had grown a little pair of back-legs each. He stared at them, and he didn't like it.

"Look here," he said to them, "you mustn't grow legs. Dear me, don't say that Artful's magic was stong magic after all. Oh, don't grow, little tadpoles!"

But they did—and they grew front legs too! Silly-One was frightened. Frogs had four legs—and now his tadpoles had, too. It was queer, very queer.

Then something happened to his caterpillars. They didn't seem well. They wouldn't eat. They all made themselves funny little cases, and tucked themselves in and went to sleep there. They couldn't be seen. Only their sleeping cases were left.

"Funny!" said Silly-One, quite alarmed. "I do hope they wake up soon. They'll starve if they don't crawl out and eat."

One day the cases moved. Silly-One watched in excitement. Now his caterpillars would come out again and eat. They had had a long, long sleep.

But, oh dear! what a dreadful shock he got—for when the cases opened, what was in them? It wasn't caterpillars! Instead there were moths, lovely yellow moths, with swallow-tails.

Silly-One stared and stared at them. Tears came into his eyes. "You've turned into moths, and I don't like you any more," he wept. "Artful's magic has changed you after all. My lovely fat caterpillars have gone."

And then he saw that his tadpoles were no longer wriggling black taddies, but tiny frogs. Yes, very very little ones, with no long tail, four little legs, and a froggy mouth. They sat on the weed at the top of the goldfish bowl, and Silly-One almost expected them to croak.

There was a knock at the door, and in came Artful, smiles all over his face. He saw the moths and the tiny frogs, and smiled even more.

"Well, wasn't my magic powerful?" he said. "Didn't I turn those tadpoles into frogs, and those caterpillars into moths? Ha, I guess you feel afraid of me now, Silly-One."

"Good-bye," said Silly-One, and tried to push Artful out of the door; but the brownie wouldn't go.

"Oh, no!" he said. "Oh, no! I haven't finished my magic yet. I'm going to change *you* into something now, Silly-One. What would you like to grow into? A moth—a frog—a bee—a beetle? Just tell me and I'll wave my wand."

"No, no," cried poor Silly-One. "Don't wave your wand at me. You are too clever, too powerful, Artful. I will come and work for you. Anyone who can change tadpoles into frogs and caterpillars into moths is a very great enchanter. I am afraid of you. Take me for your servant and treat me well."

"All right," said Artful, putting his wand away at once. "Come tomorrow. And mind—no nonsense,

Silly-One, or you'll find yourself growing wings and

feelers—and you'll be a moth flying round my lamp at night!"

Well, poor Silly-One is still Artful's servant. He didn't know that tadpoles always change into frogs, and caterpillrs always change into moths or butterflies. No, he was such a silly one.

But you knew, didn't you? You would have known it wasn't Artful's magic! Still—it does seem like very queer magic, doesn't it? How *do* tadpoles change into frogs, and caterpillars into moths or butterflies?

I don't know. Nobody knows. So perhaps it *is* magic!

Shellyback the Tortoise

WILLIAM and Suzie had a tortoise. They called him Shellyback because his back was just a big hard shell, and they liked him very much. He wandered about all over the garden and ate the grass and any rose-petals that he could find. He also ate some of Daddy's lettuces and some nice young pansy plants, which made Daddy very cross indeed.

Now, when Daddy had bought Shellyback, the man who was selling him had told Daddy that Shellyback would be most useful in the garden, and would eat up all the slugs and the beetles and caterpillars. So Daddy had been pleased, and was sure Shellyback would be a good friend.

But tortoises eat green things, not insects, which they don't like at all, so Daddy found that Shellyback wasn't so useful in the garden after all. But, as Susie said, it wasn't poor Shellyback's fault that the man who had sold him told Daddy an untruth.

"I think we'll get rid of that tortoise," Daddy said when he found that some of his lettuces had been eaten. "He's no use at all."

"But, Daddy, we like Shellyback," said William. "Really, we do. He puts his head out of his shell when we come along and looks at us so nicely out of his little brown eyes. He is a friendly creature."

"Well, I'll give him another chance," said Daddy.

So Shellyback was allowed to wander about the

garden again, and William and Susie watched to see that he did no damage. They got some wire and made him a little patch of grass of his own. They gave him a handful of rose-petals, because he

seemed to like those more than anything else. There old Shellyback lived in the sunshine, and seemed very happy indeed.

Then one autumn day he escaped and went into Daddy's seed-bed. Daddy had some nice young delphinium plants, all ready to plant out next year. He was very proud of them—and dear me, Shellyback was very foolish indeed, for he chose just those to nibble right down to the ground.

When William and Susie got home from school they hunted for Shellyback, and when they found what he had done they were most alarmed.

"Daddy will certainly make us give him away now," said William. "Those delphiniums were his pet plants. Oh, dear! Shellyback, you really are an old silly!"

The next day was Saturday. Daddy was going to spend it gardening. He went out happily into the garden and took his spade. It was good to be out in the sunshine even though the wind was frosty cold.

Daddy dug till he was tired, and then he went indoors to get his pipe. He put his hand into his pocket to get out his tobacco pouch, and discovered that his key, which he kept in the same pocket, had gone. He must have dropped it whilst he was in the garden.

"Oh, bother!" said Daddy. "That's the key of the office safe. If I lose that it is a serious matter. I shan't be able to open the safe on Monday morning. William and Susie, you must help me to look for it in the garden."

"All right, Daddy," said William. "Where do you think you may have dropped it?"

"Anywhere, almost," said Daddy. "I've been nearly all over the garden this morning. The key may have fallen out of my pocket on to the path, or on the grass, or in the beds."

"Have you been in your young delphinium bed

today?" asked Susie.

"No, why?" asked Daddy.

"Well, Daddy, we are most awfully sorry but Shellyback went there yesterday and ate your young plants." said Susie.

"What!" cried Daddy angrily. "He ate those lovely delphiniums of mine—the ones I grew from seed myself and have been watching so carefully all the summer? It's too bad! I said that tortoise must go and now he certainly must. He's a most destructive creature!"

Daddy jumped up and went striding out of doors to his young plants. When he saw his nice delphiniums nibbled right down to the roots he roared with rage.

"Where's that tortoise? I'll give him away to the milkman or the butcher or somebody this very day."

The children looked ready to cry. They knew that Shellyback certainly *would* go now.

"Go and fetch that tortoise and bring him here," said Daddy.

So off went William and Susie, but when they got to Shellyback's patch he wasn't there! He had pushed himself under the wire netting and had gone off somewhere.

They ran back to Daddy. "He's gone," they said.

"Gone?" said Daddy. "Well, he's probably eating something else of mine, then! Find him! And just hunt for my key at the same time."

The children hunted everywhere for Shellyback. They hunted under the bushes; they hunted under the hedge at the bottom of the garden; they even hunted indoors. But nowhere could the tortoise be seen. He had quite disappeared.

"Have you found him?" asked Daddy.

"No," said Susie. "We think he must have run away. Daddy. We've hunted everywhere."

"I expect he guessed he'd better make himself scarce," said Daddy. "Eating my plants like that! Now, help me to hunt for my precious key. I simply *must* find that."

Well, they hunted and they hunted for the key. But that key didn't seem to be anywhere in the garden. Like the tortoise, it had completely disappeared. Daddy was very upset.

"We must look again tomorrow," he said when the evening came and it was no use hunting any more. "I really must have it by Monday, or I may get into serious trouble at the office."

The children went to bed feeling sad. They didn't want Daddy to get into trouble, and they were unhappy because Shellyback had disappeared too. Things had gone very wrong that day!

The next day William and Susie went to the kitchen-garden to see if there were any lettuces left for a salad. As they walked round it, they saw the place where Daddy had been digging the day before. The earth looked fresh and was dug very neatly, for Daddy was a good gardener.

As William looked along the earth, he saw something strange. He stopped and looked again.

"Susie," he said, "does it seem to you as if the earth is moving just over there? Look!"

He pointed, and Susie looked. She stared in surprise. The earth certainly *was* moving. It was just like a very tiny earthquake going on in one corner.

"How funny!" said Susie. "What can it be?"

"We'd better go and see," said William. So they ran to look. The earth was heaving here and there, and little bits came up into the air every now and again.

"It's some creature burying itself," said Susie. "Whatever is it?"

William fetched a spade, and very carefully dug all round the heaving earth. And then he saw what was burying itself. Guess what it was!

"It's Shellyback the tortoise!" cried Susie in astonishment. "He's burying himself. Oh, how funny! I didn't know tortoises buried themselves, did you, William? Had we better get him out, do you think?"

Just then their next-door neighbour, Miss White, looked over the wall, and they told her what was happening.

Miss White knew all about tortoises. "Oh, yes," she said. "They always bury themselves in the ground in the winter because they don't like the cold, you know. They like to go to sleep all the winter through and wake up in the spring. If I were you I'd get him carefully out of the hole he has dug for himself and put him in a box of earth. If you leave him in the ground, Daddy may come along with his spade and crack his shell by accident when he digs over the bed. He will sleep in the box till the spring and wake up again than. Put him into a shed and he will be quite all right."

"I'm afraid Daddy is going to give him away," said Susie sadly. "But still, we'd better dig him up."

So, very carefully, the children took up old Shellyback—and as they wiped away the earth from his shell, something bright fell to the ground. William picked it up and stared at it in surprise.

"Daddy's key!" he cried. "Look, Susie; it's Daddy's lost safe-key! Oh, won't he be pleased?"

"Shellyback found it!" said Susie. "Shellyback found it! If it hadn't been for him we wouldn't have seen it. It would have lain in the ground for ever. Come and tell Daddy."

Leaving the tortoise where he was, the children raced indoors to Daddy.

"Daddy! Daddy!" they shouted. "Here's your key! Look! It was in the bit of garden that you dug over yesterday. It must have fallen out when you were digging there."

Daddy was delighted. "Oh, good!" he said. "Thank you very much, children. I am so pleased to have my key again. I know how hard you have looked for it. I would like to give you a little reward. What would you like?"

Susie and William looked at each other. They both thought of the same thing—Shellyback!

"Daddy," said William, "*we* didn't find the key, really—Shellyback did!"

"Shellyback! But I thought he had gone," said Daddy. "You said you couldn't find him."

"He *had* gone," said Susie. "He had gone to bury himself for the cold winter, and the hole he dug up was where you had dropped your key, Daddy. So when we brushed the dirt off the tortoise, your key fell to the ground."

"Well, well, well!" said Daddy.

"So, Daddy, as Shellyback found your key for you, do you think you could let us still keep him?" asked William. "Miss White says he will sleep all through the winter in a box, so he won't do any more damage now—and we will promise to make his patch so strong with wire-netting next year that he can't possibly escape to eat your plants."

"Well, you seem to have made up your minds to keep Shellyback," said Daddy; "and as he really does seem to have found my key for me, I'll reward him—and you too. You may keep him."

"Oh, thank you, Daddy!" cried the two children, and they hugged Daddy hard.

Then they ran off to find a nice box for Shellyback. They put him in, with some earth at the bottom, and carried him in the box to the shed. They put him on a shelf there, and he is sleeping soundly, quite comfy and safe in his box.